ALSO BY LILLIAN SAGE

*Sanctuary: Book One of the
Forsaken Realms Saga*

*Salvation: Book Three of the
Forsaken Realms Saga (coming soon)*

DAMNATION

BOOK TWO OF THE
FORSAKEN REALMS SAGA

LILLIAN SAGE

Avery & Co. Publishing
Chicago

DAMNATION

Book Two of the
Forsaken Realms Saga

By Lillian Sage

Published By Avery & Co. Publishing

CHICAGO, IL USA

ISBN 0-9725604-0-8

First Edition

For Frederick

TABLE OF CONTENTS

A NOTE FROM THE AUTHOR

For updates on the Forsaken Realms Saga, and to be notified when the next book is released, sign up for my free email newsletter at **LillianSage.com**

To contact me for anything else, check out my website at **LillianSage.com**

And be sure to follow me on **Facebook** at:

www.facebook.com/LillianSageAuthor

And if you enjoy this book, *please* head back to Amazon.com and leave a review. Reviews are super important for us struggling independent authors!

www.amazon.com/author/lilliansage

Thank You!
-Lillian Sage

GLOSSARY OF CHARACTERS

Alexander Graves - Ruler of the Elder Council, head of the Medai Clan, leader of the House of Graves. Lord Graves is the single most powerful vampire in the world.

Ruark Graves - Father of Alexander Graves, he was killed during the culling of the Forsaken by Natalia's father, the leader of the Forsaken.

Gabriel - Lieutenant and confidant of Alexander Graves. Gabriel acts as Alexander's second in command, helping to run the Medai's sprawling business empire.

Natalia - Exiled daughter of the leader of the Forsaken, she lives in the sewers with a band of refugee Forsaken and is their nominal leader.

Tym - Forsaken vampire and friend of Natalia. Tym is one of the oldest vampires in the world and may or may not be completely crazy.

Brenden - Forsaken vampire and member of Natalia's current family. Brenden is a hothead who burns to reunite the Forsaken.

Markus - Forsaken vampire and member of Natalia's current family. Markus is a friend of Brenden's who agreed to begin searching the world for any remaining Forsaken.

Quinn - Forsaken vampire and member of Natalia's current family. Quinn is looked upon as a sort of mother figure, or older sister by the members of Natalia's family.

Lynn - Forsaken vampire living in the sewers under London, England.

Yuri Vostrof - Member of the Elder Council, Ruler of the Morinof Clan and leader of House Vostrof, Vostrof is easily the second most powerful vampire in the world behind Alexander Graves.

Nikolai - Chief lieutenant and aide to Yuri Vostrof, Nikolai is in charge of special projects for the Morinof Clan, reporting directly to Vostrof.

Jason Grey - Twenty four year old billionaire technologist and human, Jason Grey made his fortune building social media apps before turning to cutting edge visual projection technology which has vaulted him into the ranks of the wealthiest and most powerful humans in the world.

Alain Lagarde – Ruler of the third most powerful clan, killed by Alexander in 1593.

Dominick - Steward of the London Forsaken Coven, the largest known concentration of Forsaken left in the world.

DAMNATION

CHAPTER ONE

* * *

PROLOGUE

September, 1593

Alexander Graves strode into the great hall of the castle. The most powerful rulers of the strongest Clans crowded every inch of the massive room, but all gave way before Alexander. This gathering of powerful Vampires - this Elder Council, was a new thing, and no one present knew what would happen amongst the notoriously volatile group; but one thing was certain...*Ruark was dead.*

Rain streamed down the ancient stained glass windows as thunder crackled across the night sky. *Ruark was dead.* A change was coming, though no one knew what that change would bring.

The war to annihilate the Forsaken, *Ruark's war* was going

well. The powerful leader of the Forsaken had destroyed Ruark in single-handed combat but was then killed shortly after by Morinof foot soldiers.   In fact, many of the Vampires in attendance expected Yuri Vostrof the ruler of the Morinof Clan to assume control of the Council now that Ruark was dead.

Vostrof was easily considered the second most powerful ruler after Ruark.

Though he was technically next in line to inherit his father's mantle as leader of the powerful Medai Clan and absolute head of the House of Graves, no one truly expected Ruark's son Alexander to assume his father's seat as head of the Elder Council. He was just too young; barely two hundred years old.

Reaching the dais at the head of the great hall, Alexander turned to address the gathered Vampires.

"My father is gone," intoned Alexander, "slaughtered by the hand of the Forsaken." His steely gaze swept the most powerful members of the group. "Though my father fell, the war is all but won. As you all know, the remnants of the Forsaken are being swept away as we speak. By tomorrow they will be no more."

He continued, "My father brought you together to form this Council because the Forsaken were too powerful for any one Clan to destroy on their own." a ripple of derision swept the crowd.

Alexander's voice rose to stop the murmurs. "But they proved to be as dust before our *combined* might. So now I ask you; will we disband this council..." Alexander's eyes swept the crowd again, gauging reactions. "...or will we continue, united? The Forsaken may be gone, but we do not yet stand supreme in this world. The Humans still outnumber us, unwashed and uneducated as most of them may be... I say we must come to rule them all. *It is our right!*"

The gathered Vampires broke into a clamor of argument amongst themselves. Voices drowned out voices, and Alexander stood watching, waiting for the right moment to rein them in.

Out of the rustle of voices Alain Lagarde, who many considered the most powerful Clan ruler after Vostrof strode forward. *"Young*

Alexander makes a powerful point. We must rule the humans... but who will rule us? I say that Yuri Vostrof should lead our Council."

He gestured towards Alexander and continued, "After your father, none here are more powerful in the Council. If we are to move forward together, I say the Morinof should rule." A general murmur of agreement rippled through the crowd.

Alexander moved towards Lagarde, then turned towards Vostrof, "It is true, *after the Medai* - the Morinof are the most powerful Clan. *My wife* comes from strong stock..."

The crowd fell silent and still. Everyone knew that Alexander had no wife and all wondered at the meaning of the cryptic words he had just muttered.

Vostrof smiled, sure that he had understood the veiled offer that Alexander had just delivered; Vostrof's daughter in some future marriage to Alexander in exchange for Alexander's endorsement for Yuri's leadership of the council today. He almost admired the subtlety of the offer. This youngster might be more clever than Vostrof had given him credit for. Still, if this was the price for Yuri's ascension to leadership of the Elder Council, he would gladly pay it.

Yuri's voice swept the room "A Morinof-Medai alliance would surely benefit us all," he began, "and none here are more worthy of my daughter than young Alexander. As Ruler of the Elder Council I would certainly endorse such a *future* wedding..."

Alexander locked eyes with Vostrof and then said "Your daughter Melyndra and I wed last night. She's resting comfortably at my palace surrounded by three hundred Medai soldiers who tend to her every...*comfort*."

With that, Alexander wheeled faster than human vision could comprehend, and plunged his sharply taloned fingers into the chest of Lagarde. With a sickening wrench of movement, he pulled out Alain's shriveled heart and held it high for all in the room to see.

As Lagarde's lifeless body dropped to the floor Alexander turned back to Vostrof "Your daughter and heir are *mine*...as is this Council."

Vostrof's jaw clenched tightly as

he struggled to maintain control of himself. To attack Alexander would mean the immediate death of his daughter, and while he felt nothing a human would consider *affection* for the creature whom Alexander had stolen from him and married, her death would be an irreversible loss of face for Yuri. One that he was unlikely to recover from politically, especially after the words of praise he had just spoken towards Alexander. Yuri knew that he had irrevocably lost face and was trapped.

Seeing no other options before him, Vostrof slowly knelt in front of Alexander as if in a dream and formally accepting him as leader of the Council. Within moments the entire hall were on their knees and then a thunderous cry of "*Medai!!!*"

rose from the gathered Vampires.

Alexander let the cheers roll over him for several moments then raised his head high and walked out of the hall, the new ruler of the Elder Council.

CHAPTER TWO

Rain streamed down the glass windows of Medai corporate headquarters. Deep within the building, Alexander and Natalia lay naked amongst the silk sheets of the luxurious bed they shared as often as possible.

Alexander contemplated this thing that had developed between them with no little awe. In the six hundred years of his life he had known many women, but never felt this strange pull before. It confused him.

In the months that they had been together, grabbing moments like this every few days as his schedule allowed, Alexander had begun to change. Though he would never openly acknowledge the changes within himself, or even understand that they existed,

Alexander's views had begun to shift. He was in love.

Love amongst the Forsaken was nothing new; one might even suggest that it was commonplace. But for the rest of Vampire society, love was an alien concept that simply didn't occur...*couldn't* occur.

Natalia stroked Alexander's arm as it lay draped across her chest. She was still conflicted by her emotions. By rights she should hate Alexander. After all, it was his father who had started the war that nearly annihilated her people and destroyed her own father. Since then, Alexander himself had fostered a policy of genocide towards the remnants of her people. Hunting Forsaken was still a favorite pastime for Clan members.

It was no use though, she

burned for him in ways she never thought possible. So much of her life had been about simply surviving. The weight of responsibility for the safety of her family was all she'd ever known until Alexander.

Secretly she dreamed. She dreamed of a world where her Forsaken brethren were no longer hunted. She dreamed of a world were death and fear weren't a part of everyday life. She dreamed of peace.

"You've got that distant look to your eyes again Natalia, what's on your mind?" asked Alexander.

"Nothing my love, just dreaming...it's unimportant. When can we meet again?" she answered.

"Not for some time, I'm heading out of town for a week or two on business. I'll be back as soon as I can but it may be longer than anticipated." said Alexander, "how goes the move, are your people settled?"

Natalia had recently moved her family to a new home within the sewers. The fact that they could discuss it amused her since the main reason for their need to move was Alexander and the society of aggression against her kind that he represented.

"Fine" answered Natalia "everything went smoothly, we didn't have much to move but ourselves and a few personal belongings".

Alexander grinned. Not too long ago he would have used his relationship with Natalia to root out her small pocket of followers and destroy them. At the very least he should have set his spies to discover the whereabouts of their new lair. But Alexander had done neither.

He simply felt... indifference. At least, that's what he told himself it was; just indifference. The truth was, he cared for Natalia and had no desire to hurt her or those she cared about. But Alexander wasn't quite ready to accept that reality.

"It's time for me to leave" said Alexander as he began to move towards the elevator "Be safe" he smiled.

Natalia watched him leave through the personal elevator that connected this room to his offices far above. For the hundredth time she wondered if this relationship would last...could last.

With a shrug she gathered her clothes and began the trek back to the sewers that had seemingly always been her home.

Alexander stepped out of the elevator into his sleek and modern office, silently moved to his desk and sat down. Immediately the side door opened and Gabriel walked in holding a tablet computer with a screen full of charts and financial figures.

He stopped at his customary place near Alexander's desk and waited for his lord to motion him to continue.

"What do you have for me tonight Gabriel" intoned Alexander.

"Well sire, things are quiet

tonight. The stock market was up slightly, but gold was down. Our sources tell us that the U.S. Federal Reserve will leave rates unchanged after their next meeting tomorrow, but that has already been widely expected.

Alexander nodded absent-mindedly.

"We still haven't been able to find the human Jason Grey - and his technology continues to disrupt our grip on many industries around the world..."

"Grey", mused Alexander "he must be found and destroyed; but first we need to gain control of his technology. Double your efforts Gabriel".

"Yes sire" nodded Gabriel, "Would you like me to confirm your travel plans for this morning?"

"Yes, we leave as planned" answered Alexander, "that's all for now Gabriel, return in two hours".

Gabriel bowed and walked from the room.

Alexander sat shrouded in thought. This human, this Grey was only one of the problems Alexander now faced. The Elder Council would need taken care of soon as well. Morinof planning had become more subtle as of late and Alexander was sure that some plot was underfoot - most likely aimed at himself.

The Council didn't really worry him though, there was something else that had begun to trouble Alexander and he couldn't quite put his finger on it. Something was happening in the world, something large and dangerous was coming.

Alexander could feel it in the air... like a pent up breath ready to be released...like some sort of tension about to explode.

He'd never had feelings like this before, and he seemed to be the only one who noticed it. Gabriel certainly hadn't mentioned anything like it.

The thought disturbed Alexander and he set his mind to wrestle with the problem...

CHAPTER THREE

Jason Grey sat at the expansive sleek boardroom table lost in thought. The last year had gone better than expected for him, *much better*. Once the dust had settled on his stock market manipulation and entrance into the technology industry, his personal fortune had expanded further than most people could comprehend.

Trillions, tens of trillions, even hundreds of trillions of dollars were beginning to pour into his bank accounts. More money than the tax might of most modern countries... *combined*. And there seemed to be no end in sight.

Jason's technology had disrupted more industries than even he had anticipated. Sure - he now controlled the entertainment industry, the television manufacturing industry, the cell phone industry, and other related fields. But he also began to dominate sections of the economy he hadn't even initially thought of.

Colleges were using his technology to teach classes, doctors were using it to perform exploratory surgeries with more precision than anyone had ever thought possible. Scientists were using it for modeling purposes. Nurseries were using it to entertain children.

There seemed to be few industries that weren't using his technology in some way, shape, or form. It had begun to transform the very fabric of the human race, and how they interacted and communicated with each other. It was evolutionary in every sense.

And Grey was just getting started.

Less than thirty years old, Jason had a lifetime to consolidate his grip on the world. Few people understood the true power he now held over most of the globe or what that power could be used for.

His employees now numbered in the hundreds of thousands, and would soon stretch into the millions. From Factory workers to executives, there were few castes of society who didn't work for him in some capacity.

But none of this touched his mind as he sat shrouded in thought staring at the shining table in front of him. Jason contemplated a new gamble. One that threatened everything he had built up in such a short time, but also threatened the potential lifetime he could make for himself and the near limitless power he could come to wield.

Making his final decision, he reached for the intercom button; "Send him in".

The door at the far end of the vault-like boardroom opened and a security detail half carried, half dragged the bound vampire that Jason had been holding these past months.

Jason had extracted an enormous amount of information from this creature over the course of the last few months. He now understood that there was a thriving world beneath his own world. A world controlled by these creatures; these vampires. And he understood that they were his only real threat now that the human world was virtually his for the taking.

Turning towards his captive, he declared; "I've made my decision, you have a deal. I'll release you...as soon as you turn me into one of you."

The vampire began to grin.

"My security forces have instructions to kill you though", continued Jason "at the first sign of treachery. If you plan on snapping my neck, you'll be dust moments later".

The vampire's smile froze and he began to babble fawningly "No sire, the thought never crossed my mind. I will turn you into a vampire, and you'll be a mighty vampire at that! There are none stronger than the Morinof, we will embrace you as one of our own - have no fear".

Jason knew he was taking an enormous gamble. He was tossing the dice with his own life as the stakes. But the potential was too great to ignore. As a vampire he would live forever. And with his vast wealth, he could come to rule this planet, both humans and vampires, for all eternity. It was worth the risk.

"Let's get started then." commanded Jason as his security guards began to half-carry, half-drag the vampire towards Jason.

Taking a deep breath, Jason leaned toward the vampire, extending his neck outwards.

The vampire made a sort of hissing sound as he lunged forward and bit deeply into Jason's throbbing neck. He drank deeply, but not completely and Jason's world turned to black as he slid to the floor.

The vampire moved slowly away from the body "now we wait... it shouldn't be long" he intoned.

An hour went by, then another. Suddenly Jason began to move.

He opened his eyes and was instantly disoriented. Things seemed to shift; shadows seemed to take on more shape and depth. Slowly his vision cleared and the world rushed in with a sharpness that made him gasp and nearly fall to the floor.

The sensation quickly passed and Jason took stock of himself. He held up his hands and was startled to see sharp talons slowly grow from his fingernails. He opened his mouth and felt the intrusion of fangs pierce his tongue as he bit down. A fierce strength seemed to flow through him at the same time as a painful hunger shot through his body.

Blood, he wanted blood....needed blood.

Suddenly he noticed the vampire that stood in the far corner of the room, all trace of humility and fear gone from his continence; replaced by something that could only be called hubris.

Jason walked slowly towards the vampire that was now his sire.

"Welcome child" intoned the

vampire gravely and with authority "...we have much to discuss".

"Yes we do" answered Jason as he suddenly plunged his newly taloned hand into the chest of the other vampire. As he pulled out the creature's shriveled heart, a look of utter shock crossed his face before he slumped down onto the floor...dead.

Jason glanced bemused at the shriveled heart in his hand and then casually tossed it aside. He beckoned to a member of his security team; "clean this mess up...then assemble the board, we have much to discuss".

CHAPTER FOUR

Jason drank deeply from the glass full of blood before him. He could feel the energy pulse through his body with each swallow. It was...intoxicating, so unlike anything he had experienced before. For months they had kept a steady supply of blood on-hand to keep their captive vampire fed, and now that supply would become his own, but he would need more. Much more.

Slowly and timidly the members of the Board of Grey Industries filed into the room. They were all aware of what Jason had done, but none really knew what to expect. These were Jason's closest friends and advisors, people who had been with him from the beginning. He trusted them, at least he did before he'd been turned.

When everyone was finally seated around the ornate boardroom table, Jason began.

"The experiment was a total success, I'm a vampire". The words sounded ridiculous as they came out of Jason's mouth and he smiled. The board gave a nervous chuckle.

"As far as I'm concerned, we should proceed according to plan. Are you all still resolved in our decision?"

For weeks he and the board had been discussing this incredible strategy, this plan, this...*madness*; and all had eventually agreed. Jason would turn each of the board members into vampires. Then they would turn each of their subordinates, and so on and so forth throughout Grey Industries until Jason controlled his own 'clan' of vampires that would rival - and then surpass - all the old clans in sheer numbers.

Then they would crush the other clans.

Some logistics still needed to be worked out and that was one of the reasons why Jason had called this meeting. That - and to show off his new fangs.

"The desire to follow and obey my 'master', the vampire who turned me was strong, but I was able to kill him without much effort. That tells me that we're going to need to implement some other form of control over the employees we turn. Otherwise this could get out of hand in a hurry. Any suggestions?" asked Jason.

"A kill switch?" suggested Robert Corcoran, a member of the

board who had both a technology as well as a medical background "we implant them with some sort of device that sits near their heart. Give it wifi capability so we can log in remotely to set the charge. We press a button; their heart explodes... how long were you out when you were turned?"

"Nearly two hours I think" answered Jason "we can check the security cameras for an exact time. That should be more than enough time for us to implant each new recruit...yes that's not a bad idea. Begin testing, I want a working prototype of this kill switch before we begin turning our employees".

"What about yourselves?" asked Jason "Will you submit yourself to a kill switch implantation?"

The board begin to murmur and

chatter nervously amongst themselves. Jason could smell their fear and it amused him. He began to hold each directors eye and focus his will. Slowly each director nodded agreement.

"Good" intoned Jason "I'll sleep easier then" and he smiled to try to break the tension. Keeping control of his vast army of soldiers was going to be important. From what he had pieced together from the captive, the old rulers of the clans could simply compel their subjects to do what they wanted. Something to do with power accumulated over centuries and personally turning many of their clan members. Jason wouldn't have that luxury or that kind of time.

"On to the next order of business" commanded Jason.

"We've selected those who will be turned initially; they're basically composed of those of us who have been in hiding since before we started manipulating the stock market with our short positions. Since we've all pretty much fallen off the world's radar, no one will miss us or notice that we've become vampires".

He continued "But the next wave of recruits will come from our broader holdings, our factories, and lesser subsidiaries. Those people WILL be missed. I can't have the various governments of the world suddenly looking for thousands of missing persons all linked to Grey Industries. Any suggestions?"

"We've begun sifting through personnel records," said Stacy Ng - Jason's administrative assistant. "I believe we have identified just under 2,500 loners. Employees who aren't married, don't have any immediate family to speak of and few friends; we'll start there".

"Good" intoned Jason "but we need a plan for the others. I need an army and I don't want to raise suspicions while I create it. I want a report with scenario analysis in three days".

"Is there anything else for the moment?" asked Gray as his steely eyes swept the members of his Board of Directors.

A swathe of heads nodding in the negative greeted him.

"Then let's adjourn, I need some time to think about a few things".

A little too quickly, the members of the Board of Grey Industries shuffled out of the room.

"Ah well" thought Jason "in a few days it won't matter what any of them think, or whether or not they're afraid of me".

And then he smiled.

CHAPTER FIVE

Tym walked across the barren landscape, wondering how much longer this charade would last. It had seemed like months since the voice had last returned. In all that time Tym had continued to wander aimlessly around the small desolate hunk of orb floating in nothingness.

"*Hello brother*", echoed the voice again, seemingly out of nowhere.

"You're back!" exclaimed Tym. "Where the hell have you been? I thought you said we didn't have a lot of time, I've been wandering around this cursed chunk of rock for months now!"

"Ah well, about that" chuckled the voice "time flows differently here. You haven't really been here for months, it just seems that way. Have you had any epiphanies or revelations since you've been here?"

"Revelations?! Are you kidding? I still don't know what I'm doing here, why I'm here, or what I'm supposed to do. You told me I was here to remember but I can't remember anything." muttered Tym excitedly.

"And where have you been?" prodded Tym.

"I've been here, watching you." answered the voice.

"Here?!!" shouted Tym.

"Well" chuckled the voice "...as much as you're here...I'm also somewhere else, somewhere much less pleasant than this nice little quiet spot if you must know. Frankly I'd rather be here. Of course, it's the same for you Tym, you're here and somewhere else too you know."

"Back home sleeping in my bed I

suppose?" asked Tym, some of his anger fading.

"I suppose so" answered the voice with a hint of amusement.

"Why can't I see you?" asked Tym "Can you see me?"

"I'm not entirely sure why you can't see me" answered the voice, "I can certainly see you. I suspect you'll see me when you need to".

"Great" muttered Tym.

"So why don't you explain to me again why I'm here, we're getting nowhere." prodded Tym.

"Like I said earlier General, we're here so that you can remember. It's starting to happen again and you're going to be needed." answered the voice.

"General" exclaimed Tym, confusion and uncertainty mixed throughout his voice. "What...?"

"You really don't remember anything, do you." said the voice "I wasn't sure if you really did or not. The storm...the boatman...you have no memories of what you were at all do you?"

Tym stopped walking and sat down where he stood, a look of concentration rolled across his face. That little bit of space tucked away in his brain throbbed fiercely and for a moment a wave of dizziness washed over him.

"I..." trailed off Tym as he tried to pry his way into that small nook that was locked away. Try as he might though, Tym just couldn't break through. The effort was nearly too much for him and another wave of nausea washed over him.

"You need to remember Tym,

we're running out of time..." echoed the voice.

Trying again, Tym closed his eyes as the hint of a memory rolled across his consciousness. Darkness...rain....fear. And a flash of soldiers, a sea of soldiers, as far as the eye could see. They were legion and they were watching him, waiting for his command.

Tym sucked in a sharp breath and tried to make sense of it all, but couldn't.

"I....maybe I really AM insane like everyone thinks" he muttered, utterly confused by the vision that had disappeared as quickly as it had appeared.

"What about you?" asked Tym "Do you have all your memories?"

"Yes" answered the voice "my memories are complete and always have been. Frankly I'm not really sure why you lost yours. The pit effects everyone differently I suppose."

"Well who are you then, and how do you know me?" asked Tym.

"Ah...I think we'll hold off on that story for a while, I think there's a reason why you can't see me and I don't want to upset the applecart just yet" answered the voice.

"Wait," interjected Tym "what do you mean the pit? I didn't lose my memories when I came to this place...I haven't been able to remember my past for as long as I can remember."

"This place isn't the pit..." answered the voice, and then it disappeared.

CHAPTER SIX

Marcus wandered the vast underground caverns in silence. Lately he had come to spend more and more time roaming alone in these deepest regions of the London sewers. When Brenden and he had first set out to find pockets of Forsaken, neither of them had imagined that anything like this existed. Not for the last time, he wondered if Brenden had been as successful in his search.

Markus thought back to the first day he had arrived in this Sanctuary. He'd been shocked to discover that close to seven thousand Forsaken called this place their home. It was true, Markus mused, that London was an ancient city. Over the centuries these deep regions of the sewers had been built upon time and time again; and each time the original catacombs had been pushed further beneath the Earth. What remained were vast caverns deep beneath the city that the modern world had simply forgotten about.

And here the remnants of the Forsaken had gathered, in drips and dregs much as he had. They escaped detection simply because most of them never left the safety of the deep. Hunting parties were sometimes sent up to higher regions of the sewers for food, but it was seldom necessary. The vampires here had converted old cisterns into rat farms that managed to keep most of the community steadily fed.

"I thought I'd find you down here" a voice prodded from the darkness ahead.

Markus stopped in mid-step,

slightly nonplussed by the fact that he hadn't heard this visitor arrive. "Hello Dominick, how goes it?"

Dominick was the titular head of these Forsaken, though he called himself "the Steward" for some reason instead of a Lord. Markus had gotten to know him fairly well during his time here. Dominick was voraciously curious about the outside world and appreciated everything Markus could tell him so the two of them had spent lots of time together talking.

He seemed especially curious about Markus's family; how many there were, where they lived, how they had survived. He seemed especially interested in Natalia. Though he tried to hide it, whenever they discussed her, a barely concealed excitement seemed to pour from him. Markus didn't really know what to make of it, though he had come to trust Dominick and didn't think there was anything sinister in it.

"You wander far afield today Markus, are you troubled?"

"No, just getting...restless." answered Markus "It's been nearly a year since I joined you here and I've been thinking about the rest of my family back in America. I need to tell them about you, and bring them here".

"You know that poses a bit of a problem for me, don't you?" answered Dominick.

"Why?" asked Markus.

"Well...we've survived over the centuries solely because no one knows we're down here. If even the lowliest House of the Elder Council knew about us, they'd wipe us out quickly and efficiently. There wouldn't be anything we could do to stop them...not really" answered Dominick.

"I...I guess I hadn't thought of that" said Markus. "But you've got to let me go, I've got to tell Natalia and the others about you. They need to come here."

"Well, yes...you present a special case" answered Dominick, a look of introspection on his face. "When will you leave - if I allow it?"

"I don't know," answered Markus "each day I linger here makes me more restless. It's as if I'm supposed to leave. I don't imagine that makes much sense..."

"No, not really" smiled Dominick "but I think I understand. How will you travel?"

"The same way I came, by boat. I can steal away in the hold of some cargo ship bound for the States. It shouldn't be too difficult. Those ships' holds are always teaming with rats, and no one ever bothers to slosh around in the guts of the ships. I'll be fine." answered Markus.

"And if I decided to go with you," prodded Dominick "would there be room in such a ship for me as well?"

"You?!" quipped Markus, slightly taken back by the suggestion "Why on earth would you want to come with me? And what about everyone here, you're their ruler!"

"Steward" answered Dominick automatically "I'm not the Ruler here, I'm just looking out for things until our true leader returns. Didn't we have this conversation already? You know how things work here".

"Sorry, *Steward*, I forgot...though Steward or Lord, I don't see much of a difference...but you didn't answer my question...why come with me...don't you trust me?"

"I trust you Markus, it's not that. I..." trailed off Dominick.

"Then what is it?" prodded Markus.

Dominick began to pace the cavern, his arms crossed behind his back, a look of introspection on his brow. After several moments of silent thought, he continued "Do you know how most vampires come to us?"

"I don't know" answered Markus "I never really thought about it".

"They come to us the same way you did" pointed out Dominick. "They come in dribs and drabs, sometimes one by one, sometimes in groups of two or three. We hear rumors that there are other large groups of us out there, but I've never had the kind of solid evidence you bring. Your family is small - even tiny compared to us, it's true, but compared to the trickle of Forsaken we've come across over the decades...you're quite a large group."

"One thing I've never understood" said Markus "why did you let me in here at all? I could have been a council member trying to sneak in or something, surely they're looking for you".

Dominick smiled "We have ways of determining that.

Remember that corridor you walked through the first day...that tingling you felt as you passed through the doorway? We aren't quite as technologically stunted as you might expect, there are a few of us who like to tinker with science.

"I'd forgotten about that. It burned. I meant to ask you about it when it happened but there was so much to take in that day, I guess I forgot" said Markus.

Dominick continued to pace around the cavern "Still, bringing in such a large group of outsiders such as yours poses many problems for us...detection not the least of them. If we're going to bring your family here, I need to be there to make sure everything goes well. I can't afford to put the rest of us at risk of being discovered because you were sloppy".

Markus nodded. The more he thought about it the more Dominick's words made sense. He didn't notice the mostly covered tension in Dominick's body, the not-so-hidden sense of urgency in his voice.

"Besides" joked Dominick "I've watched you get lost down here dozens of times. If we let you wander out by your own, you might never find your way back!"

Markus chuckled "I don't ever get lost...I just...lose track of where I am, that's all".

"My mistake" laughed Dominick "but seriously, I haven't been outside of this sewer for a couple hundred years. I'd like to see a bit of the world, you know?"

"My friend Brenden is like that"

answered Markus "he's always itching to get out and explore the world. It was his idea that we go looking for you guys in the first place. So when do we leave?"

"I need to make some preparations and put someone else in charge while we're gone; and in case something happens and we don't come back. I'll need at least a month or two. Do you mind waiting that long?" asked Dominick.

"Sure, I can wait that long. Natalia's going to freak out when she meets you and we tell her about all of this." answered Markus.

"I'm sure she will" answered Dominick with a strange half-smile on his face "I'm sure she will..."

CHAPTER SEVEN

Yuri Vostrof, Lord of the Morinof clan, finished feeding on the human before him. Many, if not most modern-day vampires drank their blood out of cups or glasses filled with blood harvested from one of many Morinof blood farms, but Yuri held to the old ways. He enjoyed the look of fear in these pathetic human's eyes the moment he began to feed off them. Besides, fresh organic food was always better in his opinion.

Nikolai entered through a side door and walked to his master's side.

"Ah Nikolai, good. Do you have something to report to me on our Forsaken project yet?"

"Unfortunately no my Lord" answered Nikolai gravely. "We've still received no reports from our first wave of infiltrators".

Nikolai noticed a very subtle shift in Yuri's posture. Most would have missed these warning signs but centuries of close contact gave Nikolai insight that no other vampire had. His master was angry...very angry.

"I think, my Lord, that we can only assume that our infiltrations have met with unforeseen difficulties; probably fatal ones. Given the amount of time that has elapsed, I think it's time to admit failure."

"Failure" muttered Yuri, his eyes turning flat and steely.

"Yes my lord, how would you like to proceed?" asked Nikolai.

Yuri forced down his sweeping anger and turned his mind toward the problem at hand. Several possibilities came to mind. "What do you think happened to them Nikolai? How were they detected?"

"I don't know Master. It would be inconceivable to think these ragtag Forsaken scum have any type of advanced technology that would detect our kind. Maybe they simply kill all intruders as a matter of course; I would".

"Yes," muttered Vostrof "yes that could be it. Have our surveillance teams reported anything untoward around the various perimeters?"

"No sire" answered Nikolai "everything remains quiet".

Yuri's mind roamed. Coming to control the remaining Forsaken suited his purposes perfectly, but it wasn't absolutely necessary to his overall plans. Wiping them out suited him nearly as well. But right now might not be the best time to waste his resources on it.

His stature among the Elder Council would certainly increase by finishing the job with the Forsaken where Alexander Graves hadn't.

Yuri walked a fine line. Soon he deemed that his power would equal the Medai and if a few things went his way... Yes, the time to rid the planet of that upstart fool Graves was near. Controlling the Forsaken would help achieve those goals, but destroying them would do the same thing...he simply didn't know how strong the remaining Forsaken were. Would destroying them leave him too weakened to finish off the Medai?

And then there was this new human to deal with, this Jason

Grey. His technology had come to disrupt many Morinof ventures. Yuri could only hope that the Medai were having as many difficulties with him.

"Tell me about the human" prodded Yuri.

"Grey, yes. Unfortunately sire I have nothing else to report on him since the last time we discussed it. Our assassin has not checked in. We can only assume that he was caught and destroyed by the human. His security forces are rumored to be growing at an alarming rate." answered Nikolai.

"Imbeciles!" screamed Yuri "How can I be expected to function when I'm surrounded by Imbeciles!"

Nikolai stood rock still and silent. He'd seen his master fly into too many violent rages over the years to offer any answer.

"Leave me Nikolai" hissed Vostrof.

Nikolai moved quickly to the door and back to the relative safety of his own office, leaving Vostrof seething behind him.

Yuri would have to move sooner than he had planned. Graves and the Medai must be crushed soon. Only then could Vostrof consolidate his power completely over the Elder Council. He would need their combined might in order to deal with this new human.

But first things first, he would need to destroy the remaining Forsaken. Only that action would give him the standing he needed to usurp Graves in the Council, and only after removing Graves from his overlordship of the Council could Yuri reasonably expect to stamp out the Medai.

Settling back into his overturned chair, Yuri's mind began to churn possibilities and formulate a plan...

CHAPTER EIGHT

Alexander sat behind the desk in his sleek and modern office pouring over rows of figures as they rolled across the screen in front of him.

Things were bad. Very bad.

Ever since Jason Grey had appeared on the scene, Medai stock market holdings had plummeted. That was bad enough, but now whole companies controlled by Alexander were beginning to flounder.

Several lesser subsidiaries were on the verge of bankruptcy and others were sliding quickly into dangerous territory.

There was very little Alexander could do to stem the tide. Grey's technology had rendered so many industries obsolete - it amounted to wholesale economic carnage.

The best Alexander could hope to do was cut his losses and consolidate his cash position.

But where to put his cash? Grey had begun to secretly purchase majority holdings in many of the major world banks through an ingenious network of nominees that the Medai spy network had only just discovered.

Making a decision, Alexander pushed a button and Gabriel entered the room.

"Yes my lord?" intoned Gabriel.

"Instruct our brokers to begin selling our entire stock portfolio. Spread it around as much as possible so as not to rock the market. I want the best possible price – all things considered."

"Yes sire".

"Convert 80% of the proceeds

into gold and store it in our vaults. Spread it around Gabriel; I want half of it here on level 4, then spread the rest equally across the vaults in our various headquarter buildings...Europe, Asia, and South America" ordered Alexander.

Gabriel's fingers worked across the ever present tablet making notes.

"We can take some solace in the fact that the Morinof are probably having just as a bad a time of it as we are" muttered Alexander.

"We can hope so" agreed Gabriel.

Alexander stared off into space. The loss of income was worrisome, but there was something else troubling him...something larger. Try as he might though, he couldn't put his finger on it.

"There's a pattern here" muttered Alexander.

"My lord?" inquired Gabriel.

"Grey...there's a pattern to what he's doing...I can *feel* it. But I can't decipher the pattern. There's something..."

Gabriel nodded, though he clearly didn't understand.

"Is there anything I can do, my lord?" asked Gabriel.

"No, no. That's all Gabriel" answered Alexander. Gabriel turned and strode away to begin implementing the stock market sell orders.

Over the centuries Alexander had uncovered countless attempts to destroy his house and clan. Rivalry ran deep among the Elder Council – assassination attempts were an everyday part of his existence. But this was different. This was deeper, more complicated, and more subtle. The world was shifting and Alexander feared the tidal wave would destroy not just his house and clan but possibly the entire Elder Council.

It was little more than a feeling, but it was a feeling that continued to grow steadily each day. Momentous things were happening in the wide world...and Alexander was powerless to stop them. The feeling infuriated him.

CHAPTER NINE

The last two months had been a flurry of activity amongst the London Forsaken. Dominick seemed to have a thousand things to do and not enough time to do any of them. Markus didn't really understand what the fuss was all about. He was simply going home to America and Dominick was coming with him.

What was so complicated about that?

When he first asked what all the fuss was about, Dominick blew him off.

"Oh you know, I just need to make preparations in case something happens to me and I don't return. You never know what could happen out there!" explained Dominick.

But as the weeks wore by, Markus realized that something else was happening. It was as if the entire society was mobilizing. Everyone seemed to be on high alert, and there was a momentous feeling in the air.

Markus didn't understand it.

Now the two of them sat deep in the soggy holds of a cargo ship headed towards America. There were plenty of rats to live on and Dominick didn't seem to mind the fare. The Forsaken of lower London lived off of the rats that were so prevalent in the sewers, in fact they had grown massive rat farms deep in the forgotten cisterns of the ancient city.

"You've been in contact with your family?" asked Dominick for the fourth time.

"Yes, I told you three times yes. Natalia moved our family to another part of the city for some reason or another, I don't understand why. But she gave me directions and I won't have any trouble finding the place" answered Markus.

"And you didn't tell her about me, like we discussed?" asked Dominick.

"Well...I mean..." said Markus.

"I thought we understood each other Markus!" shot Dominick. "My safety demands secrecy!"

"I know, I know. It's just...well you know," answered Markus "It's Natalia...I had to tell her something. I couldn't just show up with a stranger like that."

"What exactly did you tell her Markus?"

"Just that I had found some of our brethren and that one of them was returning with me. I didn't tell her anything else...you can still have your little surprise or whatever this is all about".

Dominick began to pace, lost in thought. "Yes that might be ok," he replied.

"Sit down man, you're sloshing water all over the place" quipped Markus. They were deep in the hold of the ship, and like all cargo ships, this one seemed to leak constantly.

"I'm sorry Markus, it's just that I worry. Nothing like this has happened in all the years we've been hiding. I don't want anything to go wrong and I don't want to put any of us in danger".

"I know, I know" answered Markus "I've heard you say that a hundred time. Everything is going to be ok".

"Just be careful, that's all I'm saying", suggested Alexander as he looked down at Natalia sprawled across the bed.

"What do you mean?" asked Natalia "Markus said he's bringing one of our brethren back home with us. He's not one of yours is he?"

"No," answered Alexander, "not a Clan Member so far as I know. That doesn't mean he poses no threat to you..."

"How can one Forsaken pose a threat to us? Markus vouches for him and I trust Markus".

"Trust," mused Alexander "a novel concept".

"Have you decided what to do about your Jason Grey problem?" asked Natalia as she stretched luxuriously in the large sleek bed.

"Yes," answered Alexander "and I'll need your help".

"My help?" quipped Natalia, slightly startled "what can I possibly do to help?"

"Not you, but the Forsaken..." answered Alexander cryptically. "Will you come talk to me after you've met with Markus? I'll explain everything then".

Natalia nodded, confusion playing across her brow, "if you insist..."

"These are momentous times my love" answered Alexander, "and they call for drastic measures.

Something big is happening in the world. Big, and...dark. It fills me with a sense of foreboding that I've never felt before".

"I've felt it too" answered Natalia "something is changing, something is...*shifting*. I can't describe it any better than that".

Alexander looked deep into Natalia's eyes "I know you feel it too... I think not many of us will make it through what's coming..."

"I know" answered Natalia.

Three days later Markus and Dominick stood outside the entrance to the sewers that Natalia and her family called home. Markus began to walk forward.

"Wait," shot Dominick as he

reached out and grabbed Markus by the forearm "give me a minute".

"Nothing to be nervous about man, they're waiting inside. Let's go!" answered Markus.

Dominick was clearly nervous, which was odd for a vampire, but then again Forsaken were an odd bunch who could manifest emotion in different ways.

Markus didn't put much into it, so excited he was to be home and see his family. He wondered if Brenden had returned as well.

"Alright," said Dominick after taking a long deep breath, "let's go".

Markus walked through the entrance, down the tunnel and into the adjoining room where his family awaited their arrival.

As he walked through the door he saw his brethren scattered about the large room, and there in the middle stood Natalia, stock still and cold as ice.

Dominick pushed ahead of Markus and into the room, eyes only for Natalia he rushed in and threw himself onto the ground at her feet. Tears streamed down his face as he looked up from his prostrations "It's true!" he have gasped, half sobbed; the sound a triumphant blast through the room.

Natalia stood stock still, jaw clenched tightly as she looked down at the fawning form of Dominick at her feet.

"Dominick..." she muttered...

"Shit"

CHAPTER TEN

The rulers of the Elder Council began to file into the large sleek boardroom of Medai headquarters for this meeting.

It had been several years since they had all met in one place, but these were troubling circumstances.

Each House of each Clan had recently felt the economic effects of Grey Industries. What started out as a nuisance had quickly become a catastrophe as Grey's grip on the world economy had only tightened. Something had to be done and the rulers of the major Clans looked to Alexander for answers.

Yuri Vostrof strode toward the boardroom door, his lieutenant and chief aide Nikolai a half step behind him. Both fought to keep the anticipation from their faces as they contemplated the plan that they had put into place and were about to enact. After all these long years, the upstart Alexander would finally be removed from this earth.

Several weeks earlier Vostrof had discovered Alexander's relationship with Natalia. At first he had been shocked to discover the heir of the Forsaken still lived, but that shock paled in comparison to the jolt he felt upon discovering that Alexander shared his bed with her.

When word of this treason reached the Elder Council, Alexander would be eviscerated... *literally.* Yuri's ascension as Ruler of the Elder Council was guaranteed.

Yuri had been amused to discover that Alexander had called this emergency meeting. It would be the perfect time for Yuri to announce Alexander's treason and assume leadership of the Council.

Yuri was so excited that he failed to notice the two guards standing outside the boardroom door until they barred his entrance.

"Forgive us your Lordship, but we've been instructed to allow entrance to Rulers only... no aides!" barked the guard.

"What is this!" hissed Yuri. "Nikolai is my right arm, he goes where I go!"

"Apologies Lord Morinof, due to the nature of this meeting and the... ah... delicate sensitivity of the discussions, Lord Alexander has declared that only Rulers shall enter", answered the guard; "all the others have agreed and await you inside".

Yuri started, if everyone else had already agreed there was little he could do; and truly Nikolai's presence wasn't necessary for what was about to happen.

"Very well", exclaimed Yuri with as much grandeur as he could muster as he swept past the guard into the room, leaving Nikolai to wait in the adjoining antechamber with all the other lieutenants and heirs.

As the second most powerful Lord after Alexander, it was Yuri's prerogative to enter last and as he crossed the floor he noticed the thinly veiled trepidation in the eyes of the assembled vampires.

Settling down into the last remaining large, overstuffed, thrown-like chair near the head of the table Yuri began to collect himself as he contemplated his opening move.

Moments later a side door opened and Alexander strode into the room and took his place at the head of the table.

"We come here today to discuss the growing threat of Jason Grey" began Alexander "and to discuss my plan to destroy him..."

"Yes!" exclaimed Yuri, "but first I have some startling news that the Council must needs hear".

"..ah yes Yuri, thank you. I had nearly forgotten" chuckled Alexander "let me begin for you."

Before Yuri could speak Alexander continued "for some time now I have been sharing my bed with Natalia, the heir of the Forsaken..."

Voices broke out amongst the assembled Vampires but Alexander over-rode them "...in an attempt to discover and infiltrate their remaining stronghold...I have succeeded entirely in discovering their location."

Alexander continued, "It turns out, their numbers are far greater than any of us had anticipated".

"You...you did it on purpose?" stammered Yuri "to smoke them out?"

"Of course" smirked Alexander, knowing that Yuri had planned to use this information to unseat and destroy him and enjoying the discomfort evident on Yuri's face.

"The eminent downfall of the Forsaken is clearly interesting, but first we need to discuss the more pressing threat of Jason Grey", continued Alexander.

"Like the threat of the Forsaken ages ago, this Grey has grown too strong for any of us to destroy on our own," declared Alexander "to that end I have decided that we must all join together once again to defeat him".

Yuri broke in "but we are joined already, that's why this council exists, that's why we're here today".

"Correct, answered Alexander "but the loose alliance of the past will no longer serve. I have decided to remove each of you and assume direct control of each of your Houses".

Before anyone could open their mouths to protest, lightning fast wooden stakes shot through the back of each chair around the conference table, through the backs and into the hearts of each occupant. The assembled Vampires barely had time to register the shock on their faces as their bodies turned to ash and fell away to nothingness. Slowly the wooden stakes retracted back into the backs of the chairs and Alexander sat motionless staring at the blank seats around him, dust still scattered about. He allowed himself a moment to remember the centuries that Yuri Vostrof had plotted against him. He would almost miss the rivalry, but in the end knew that this could only have ended this way.

The side door opened and Gabriel walked in, "That was quick sire..."

"Yes," answered Alexander "now the hard part begins. Send in the lieutenants".

Gabriel tapped on his ever present tablet computer and the

main door opened and the lieutenants and heirs to every major House of the Council entered, confusion and uncertainty written on their faces.

"Come in my Lords," intoned Alexander, "Have a seat. We have grave matters to discuss".

The incoming vampires glanced at the piles of ash on the seats of each chair and immediately knew what had happened. They also knew what was likely to happen to each of them if they sat in the same chairs.

Alexander sat without fear. Though he looked vulnerable sitting in his chair at the head of the table, he knew that a safety screen would enfold him should any of the waiting vampires move to destroy him. Alexander had left nothing to chance.

"Yes, I have destroyed your Masters...each and every one of them. But *you* have nothing to fear. If I wanted you dead none of you would have left the antechamber. Sit, we have much to discuss".

The uncertain vampires began to take their seats.

Once everyone was seated, Alexander began... "As I'm sure you're all aware, Jason Grey and his technology have become a direct threat to us all economically, but the threat is much greater than any of us had imagined."

Alexander continued, "Our intelligence now tells us that Grey has been turned, by whom - we don't know. More worrying is the fact that he's began building an army of vampires under his direct control."

Alexander reached into his breast pocket and removed a small device. With a flick of his wrist he dropped it on the table.

"Sources confirm that he's implanting his children with this kill switch. He places it next to their hearts. With a tap of his mobile phone, a wi-fi signal is sent to the switch and the heart explodes. That's how he controls his people since he doesn't have the power yet to compel them mentally. Any attempt to remove the device triggers it; resulting in instant death."

The vampires began to mutter around the table.

Alexander continued "Grey's plan is simple. With his money and his power he will soon have an army that equals our combined might...if left unchecked his army could soon dwarf ours in size. He plans on destroying us completely, then ruling this planet forever. Eventually he'll simply enslave the human race, keeping just enough of them alive to keep his blood banks supplied and running".

A stunned silence stretched over the room.

"Already his army is too large for any one of our Clans; united we may have some chance. But we need to be united in a way unlike our old loose alliance."

Alexander continued, "Our old petty squabbling and feuding could only hurt us going forward. I decided it was time to wipe the slate clean."

Alexander chuckled almost to

himself, "Of course, the only way to do that was to destroy each and every one of your Masters".

"Each of you will be implanted with one of these kill switches today..."

The assembled group began to protest but Alexander's voice rose, "Failure to comply will be met with instant death".

The group began to quiet down. None had any illusions about leaving here alive. If their Master's couldn't outwit Alexander then how could they?

"I name each of you Lord of your respective Houses, but you will all answer to me. My orders will be carried out exactly and immediately or I'll flip your switch and you'll be dead faster than your Master died. Do we understand each other?"

Alexander caught the eye of every Vampire present and assessed each of them.

"Good," intoned Alexander, "We'll begin coordinating Command and Control for the upcoming War with Grey as soon as your kill switches are in place. That is all".

Gabriel motioned to the main door, "If you'll all follow me to the surgical rooms, we will begin immediately..."

EPILOGUE

"Do you believe in God Tym?" the voice echoed out of the air surrounding him.

"God?" answered Tym, surprise in his voice "You're not serious are you?"

"What's strange about that question?" replied the voice "You're a vampire, certainly you're not human. Surely you came from somewhere. You can't tell me you don't believe there's something else out there. Something spiritual. You have preternatural senses, you can already see a whole other world that humans could never comprehend."

He continued, "Yet many humans, if not most humans, believe in God or some form of higher power. And you don't?"

"It's not that I don't believe in

God" answered Tym, "It's just that I never really gave it much thought. I guess I always figured those scared humans had merely perceived us in some way. What they consider God was probably just one of us messing with them".

The voice chuckled, "Well think about it a little bit. I can tell you that God does exist and I'm a little surprised that you don't believe already...but then again, I suppose you did lose your memories".

"My memories?" laughed Tym "what do my memories have to do with me believing in God? You aren't going to tell me that I've met him or something".

"No Tym" chuckled the voice "as far as I know you've never met God, that's not what I meant."

"What did you mean then?"

asked Tym.

"I don't know...just trying to prod those memories of yours. Frankly, I don't really know what else to do with you. I assumed you'd regain your memories when we got here, or shortly thereafter. This waiting is starting to worry me."

"You?!" exclaimed Tym, "How do you think I feel!?"

"Good point" answered the voice.

Tym began to pace around again. It was becoming more and more obvious that something needed to be done. He couldn't just sit here for the rest of eternity. Yet Tym didn't know what to do.

He began to scan the area around him. Over the last few months...or at least what he perceived to be the last few months...Tym had scoured every inch of his surroundings. There wasn't much to see; in fact there wasn't anything to see...

...Nothing except a decent sized rock sitting on the ground. It wasn't large enough to warrant attention, really only slightly large enough to sit on. Tym had checked it out the first day he had arrived and walked past it several times since then. There was nothing mysterious about it, no secret passage underneath it, nothing at all to even consider. But yet...

Tym began to walk towards the stone. His head continued to buzz; always that buzzing deep within the far corner of his mind. It was time for Tym to unlock those memories, and since the only tool he had was a large rock, Tym resolved to smash his head against it until he remembered.

"What are you doing" echoed the voice as Tym walked purposefully towards the rock.

"Oh nothing, I'm just going to bash my head against this rock until I start to remember."

"You're going to do WHAT?" exclaimed the voice.

"You heard me...do you have a better idea?" answered Tym as he made his way towards the rock.

"Tym, that's the stupidest thing I've ever heard. Bashing your head against a rock isn't going to help anything." said the voice.

"Why not?" answered Tym, "Something's obviously locked away in my brain. Neither of us can think of any logical way to get it out...we might as well turn towards the illogical. Besides, this rock's gotta be here for some reason, right?"

With that Tym made his way next to the stone and prepared himself. Getting down on his knees he rocked back and forth a little bit, testing the environment and his leverage.

"Here goes nothing" he exclaimed and threw his head back with as much force as he could muster, intent on whipping it forward to crush his forehead against the side of the rock.

Suddenly Tym stopped, mid head-swing, as the rock disappeared in a flash. In its place stood a large pedestal upon which sat an ancient and opened book.

Tym looked down and noticed

that it was an old copy of the Bible, something he had never read before but was oddly familiar with.

As he looked down, one of the passages seemed to glow and he found that he couldn't look away.

"What is it?" asked the voice, gravely.

"Genesis, chapter 6 verse 4..." answered Tym, a slight tremble to his voice...

"The Nephilim were on the earth in those days--and also afterward--when the sons of God went to the daughters of humans and had children by them. They were the heroes of old, men of renown."

Suddenly the world exploded before Tym's eyes and memories began to flood one on top of the other through his conscious mind. Tym's eyes widened and his stomach churned as he dropped to the ground.

His past rushed before his eyes like a movie and he *remembered...*

The sky rolled with endless deep, dark clouds. Tym's seemingly limitless army stretched behind him as far as the eye could see and he felt an overwhelming sense of pride at their numbers and strength but at the same time a growing sense of panic, even fear as the rain continued to fall. So much rain.

His army were the heroes of old - the warriors of renown; whom mankind first named the Nephilim...and later; Vampire. Tym was their General. In the early days, when the Sons of God lay with the daughters of man, they begot the Nephilim — half angel, half human. Compared to humans they seemed like giants and contained powers mere mortals couldn't imagine. And they had multiplied in strength and number through the years until they far outnumbered the humans.

No one knew exactly when it had happened, but eventually the Nephilim had merely decided to rid the world of the weak humans; to wipe them off the planet without mercy. They had forgotten their own history, their own ancestry…And they had forgotten that God was watching.

Their war had very nearly succeeded. The combined armies of humanity had met them head on in combat but could not withstand the staggering might of their destroyers. But not all of humanity had fought, one human had stayed behind with his family…building a boat.

Now the rains continued to fall as

Tym's mighty host marched toward the last remaining human, who called himself Noah. But Tym knew they wouldn't reach him before the flood waters overcame them.

Tym seethed with impotent fury. To stop their march and simply wait for death was inconceivable; but to continue marching was pointless. Failure burned deep within Tym as he motioned his army forward.

Tym shook his head as memories and emotions crashed about, threatening to overwhelm him.

"Now you understand" muttered the voice.

Tym turned toward the voice and saw that the voice was no longer just a voice. In its place stood a magnificent creature, nearly eight feet tall and a piercing white light shone through every inch of it's being and gigantic wings – nearly fifty feet each hung poised from his shoulders.

"Hello brother" smiled the creature, "or should I say *half* brother..."

Tym looked on in amazement, memories flooding back into his mind.

"It's happening again brother" said the creature "the Nephilim are trying to wipe out the human race..."

Tym nodded, "and we're going to stop them?"

The creature smiled..."It's time to make amends for your past transgressions. It's time to save the Humans and put what's wrong right again...Yes brother, we're going to stop them."

THE END

Can I Ask You A Quick Favor?

If you enjoyed this book, _please_ head back to Amazon.com and leave a review.

Reviews are incredibly important for us small independent writers. Even one or two positive reviews can vault our books to the top of the search results at Amazon.

www.amazon.com/author/lilliansage

And would you share the book on Facebook or Twitter too? Let's get the word out!! ☺

GET YOUR NAME IN MY NEXT BOOK

As a thank you for leaving a Review on Amazon, I'd like to print your name on a thank you page in the paperback version of the next book in this series.

Just head to **LillianSage.com** and use the contact form to drop me an email. Point me toward the review you left and give me the name you'd like me to print in the book.

I really appreciate it.

Thank You!
-Lillian

**BOOK THREE OF THE
FORSAKEN REALMS SAGE:**

If you enjoyed this book and would like to be notified the moment the next one is released, then head over to:

LillianSage.com

Just fill out the contact form and you'll be signed up for my mailing list. I'll send you an email when the next book is out.

While you're there, check out the website, chat with other fans, send me email and whatever.

And be sure to follow me on **Facebook**, and **Twitter** at:

Facebook.com/LillianSageAuthor